The Munschworks Grand Treasury

The Munschworks Grand Treasury

stories by **Robert Munsch and Michael Kusugak**
illustrations by
**Michael Martchenko, Hélène Desputeaux and
Vladyana Langer Krykorka**

annick press
toronto • new york • vancouver

© **2001 Munschworks Grand Treasury (Annick Press Ltd.)**
Munschworks © 1998 Annick Press Ltd.
Munschworks 2 © 1999 Annick Press Ltd.
Munschworks 3 © 2000 Annick Press Ltd.
Cover illustration by Michael Martchenko
Ninth printing, June 2010

We acknowledge the support of the Canada Council for the Arts, the Ontario Arts Council, and the Government of Canada through the Book Publishing Industry Development Program (BPIDP) for our publishing activities.

Cataloging in Publication Data
Munsch, Robert N., 1945-
  The Munschworks grand treasury

ISBN 1-55037-685-3

I. Kusugak, Michael. II. Martchenko, Michael. III. Desputeaux, Hélène.
IV. Krykorka, Vladyana. V. Title.

PS8576.U575M86 2001   jC813'.54   C2001-930060-3
PZ7.M927Mu 2001

The art in this book was rendered in watercolor.
The text was typeset in Century Oldstyle and Adlib.

Distributed in Canada by: Published in the U.S.A. by Annick Press (U.S.) Ltd.
Firefly Books Ltd.   Distributed in the U.S.A. by:
66 Leek Crescent   Firefly Books (U.S.) Inc.
Richmond Hill, ON   P.O. Box 1338
L4B 1H1   Ellicott Station
                      Buffalo, NY 14205

Printed and bound in China.

visit us at: **www.annickpress.com**
visit Robert Munsch at: **www.robertmunsch.com**

Contents

The Paper Bag Princess

by Robert Munsch
illustrated by
Michael Martchenko

Elizabeth was a beautiful princess. She lived in a castle and had expensive princess clothes. She was going to marry a prince named Ronald.

Unfortunately, a dragon smashed her castle, burned all her clothes with his fiery breath, and carried off Prince Ronald.

Elizabeth decided to chase the dragon and get Ronald back.

She looked everywhere for something to wear, but the only thing she could find that was not burnt was a paper bag. So she put on the paper bag and followed the dragon.

He was easy to follow, because he left a trail of burnt forests and horses' bones.

Finally, Elizabeth came to a cave with a large door that had a huge knocker on it. She took hold of the knocker and banged on the door.

The dragon stuck his nose out of the door and said, "Well, a princess! I love to eat princesses, but I have already eaten a whole castle today. I am a very busy dragon. Come back tomorrow."

He slammed the door so fast that Elizabeth almost got her nose caught.

Elizabeth grabbed the knocker and banged on the door again.

The dragon stuck his nose out of the door and said, "Go away. I love to eat princesses, but I have already eaten a whole castle today. I am a very busy dragon. Come back tomorrow."

"Wait," shouted Elizabeth. "Is it true that you are the smartest and fiercest dragon in the whole world?"

"Yes," said the dragon.

"Is it true," said Elizabeth, "that you can burn up ten forests with your fiery breath?"

"Oh, yes," said the dragon, and he took a huge, deep breath and breathed out so much fire that he burnt up fifty forests.

"Fantastic," said Elizabeth, and the dragon took another huge breath and breathed out so much fire that he burnt up one hundred forests.

"Magnificent," said Elizabeth, and the dragon took another huge breath, but this time nothing came out. The dragon didn't even have enough fire left to cook a meatball.

Elizabeth said, "Dragon, is it true that you can fly around the world in just ten seconds?"

"Why, yes," said the dragon, and jumped up and flew all the way around the world in just ten seconds.

He was very tired when he got back, but Elizabeth shouted, "Fantastic, do it again!"

So the dragon jumped up and flew around
the whole world in just twenty seconds.
When he got back he was too tired to talk,
and he lay down and went straight to sleep.

Elizabeth whispered, very softly, "Hey, dragon." The dragon didn't move at all.

She lifted up the dragon's ear and put her head right inside. She shouted as loud as she could, "Hey, dragon!"

The dragon was so tired he didn't even move.

Elizabeth walked right over the dragon and opened the door to the cave.

There was Prince Ronald. He looked at her and said, "Elizabeth, you are a mess! You smell like ashes, your hair is all tangled and you are wearing a dirty old paper bag. Come back when you are dressed like a real princess."

"Ronald," said Elizabeth, "your clothes are really pretty and your hair is very neat. You look like a real prince, but you are a bum."

They didn't get married after all.

The Fire Station

by Robert Munsch
illustrated by Michael Martchenko

*M*ichael and Sheila were walking down the street. As they passed the fire station Sheila said, "Michael! Let's go ride a fire truck."

"Well," said Michael, "I think maybe I should ask my mother, and I think maybe I should ask my father and I think maybe..."

"I think we should go in," said Sheila. Then she grabbed Michael's hand and pulled him up to the door.

Sheila knocked: BLAM – BLAM – BLAM – BLAM – BLAM. A large fireman came out and asked, "What can I do for you?"

"Well," said Michael, "maybe you could show us a fire truck and hoses and rubber boots and ladders and all sorts of stuff like that."

"Certainly," said the fireman.

"And maybe," said Sheila, "you will let us drive a fire truck?"

"Certainly not," said the fireman.

They went in and looked at ladders and hoses and big rubber boots. Then they looked at little fire trucks and big fire trucks and enormous fire trucks. When they were done Michael said, "Let's go."

"Right," said Sheila. "Let's go into the enormous fire truck."

While they were in the truck, the fire alarm went off: CLANG – CLANG – CLANG – CLANG – CLANG.

"Oh, no!" said Michael.

"Oh, yes!" said Sheila. Then she grabbed Michael and pulled him into the back seat.

Firemen came running from all over. They slid down poles and ran down stairs. Then they jumped onto the truck and drove off. The firemen didn't look in the back seat. Michael and Sheila were in the back seat.

They came to an enormous fire. Lots of yucky-colored smoke got all over everything. It colored Michael yellow, green and blue. It colored Sheila purple, green and yellow.

When the fire chief saw them he said, "What are you doing here!"

Sheila said, "We came in the fire truck. We thought maybe it was a bus. We thought maybe it was a taxi. We thought maybe it was an elevator. We thought maybe..."

"I think maybe I'd better take you home," said the fire chief. He put Michael and Sheila in his car and drove them away.

When Michael got home he knocked on the door. His mother opened it and said, "You messy boy! You can't come in and play with Michael! You're too dirty." She slammed the door right in Michael's face.

"My own mother," said Michael. "She didn't even know me." He knocked on the door again.

His mother opened the door and said, "You dirty boy! You can't come in and play with Michael. You're too dirty. You're absolutely filthy. You're a total mess. You're...Oh, my!...Oh, no!...YOU'RE MICHAEL!"

Michael went inside and lived in the bathtub for three days until he got clean.

When Sheila came home she knocked on the door. Her father opened it and saw an incredibly messy girl. He said, "You can't come in to play with Sheila. You're too dirty." He slammed the door right in her face.

"Ow," said Sheila. "My own father and he didn't even know me."

She kicked and pounded on the door as loudly as she could. Her father opened the door and said, "Now stop that racket, you dirty girl. You can't come in to play with Sheila. You're too dirty. You're absolutely filthy. You're a total mess. You're...Oh, my!...Oh, no!... YOU'RE SHEILA!"

"Right," said Sheila, "I went to a fire in the back of a fire truck and I got all smoky. I WASN'T EVEN SCARED."

Sheila went inside and lived in the bathtub for five days until she got clean.

Then Michael took Sheila on a walk past the police station. He told her, "If you ever take me in another fire truck, I am going to ask the police to put you in jail."

"JAIL!" yelled Sheila. "Let's go look at the jail! What a great idea!"

"Oh, no!" yelled Michael, and Sheila grabbed his hand and pulled him into the police station.

I Have to Go!

by Robert Munsch
illustrated by Michael Martchenko

One day Andrew's mother and father were taking him to see his grandma and grandpa. Before they put him in the car his mother said, "Andrew, do you have to go pee?"

Andrew said, "No, no, no, no, no."

His father said, very slowly and clearly, "Andrew, do you have to go pee?"

"No, no, no, no," said Andrew. "I have decided never to go pee again."

So they put Andrew into the car, fastened his seatbelt and gave him lots of books, and lots of toys, and lots of crayons, and drove off down the road—VAROOMMM. They had been driving for just one minute when Andrew yelled, "I HAVE TO GO PEE!"

"YIKES," said the father.

"OH NO," said the mother.

Then the father said, "Now, Andrew, wait just five minutes. In five minutes we will come to a gas station where you can go pee."

Andrew said, "I have to go pee RIGHT NOW!"

So the mother stopped the car—SCREEEEECH. Andrew jumped out of the car and peed behind a bush.

When they got to Grandma's and Grandpa's house, Andrew wanted to go out to play. It was snowing, and he needed a snowsuit. Before they put on the snowsuit, the mother and the father and the grandma and the grandpa all said, "ANDREW! DO YOU HAVE TO GO PEE?"

Andrew said, "No, no, no, no, no."

So they put on Andrew's snowsuit. It had five zippers, 10 buckles and 17 snaps. It took them half an hour to get the snowsuit on.

Andrew walked out into the back yard, threw one snowball and yelled, "I HAVE TO GO PEE."

The father and the mother and the grandma and the grandpa all ran outside, got Andrew out of the snowsuit and carried him to the bathroom.

When Andrew came back down they had a nice long dinner. Then it was time for Andrew to go to bed.

Before they put Andrew into bed, the mother and the father and the grandma and the grandpa all said, "ANDREW! DO YOU HAVE TO GO PEE?"

Andrew said, "No, no, no, no, no."

So his mother gave him a kiss, and his father gave him a kiss, and his grandma gave him a kiss, and his grandpa gave him a kiss.

"Just wait," said the mother, "he's going to yell and say he has to go pee."

"Oh," said the father, "he does it every night. It's driving me crazy."

The grandmother said, "I never had these problems with my children."

They waited for five minutes, 10 minutes, 15 minutes, 20 minutes.

The father said, "I think he is asleep."

The mother said, "Yes, I think he is asleep."

The grandmother said, "He is definitely asleep and he didn't yell and say he had to go pee."

Then Andrew said, "I wet my bed."

So the mother and the father and the grandma and the grandpa all changed Andrew's bed and Andrew's pajamas. Then the mother gave him a kiss, and the father gave him a kiss, and the grandma gave him a kiss, and the grandpa gave him a kiss, and the grownups all went downstairs.

They waited five minutes, 10 minutes, 15 minutes, 20 minutes, and from upstairs Andrew yelled, "GRANDPA, DO YOU HAVE TO GO PEE?"

And Grandpa said, "Why, yes, I think I do."

Andrew said, "Well, so do I."

So they both went to the bathroom and peed in the toilet, and Andrew did not wet his bed again that night, not even once.

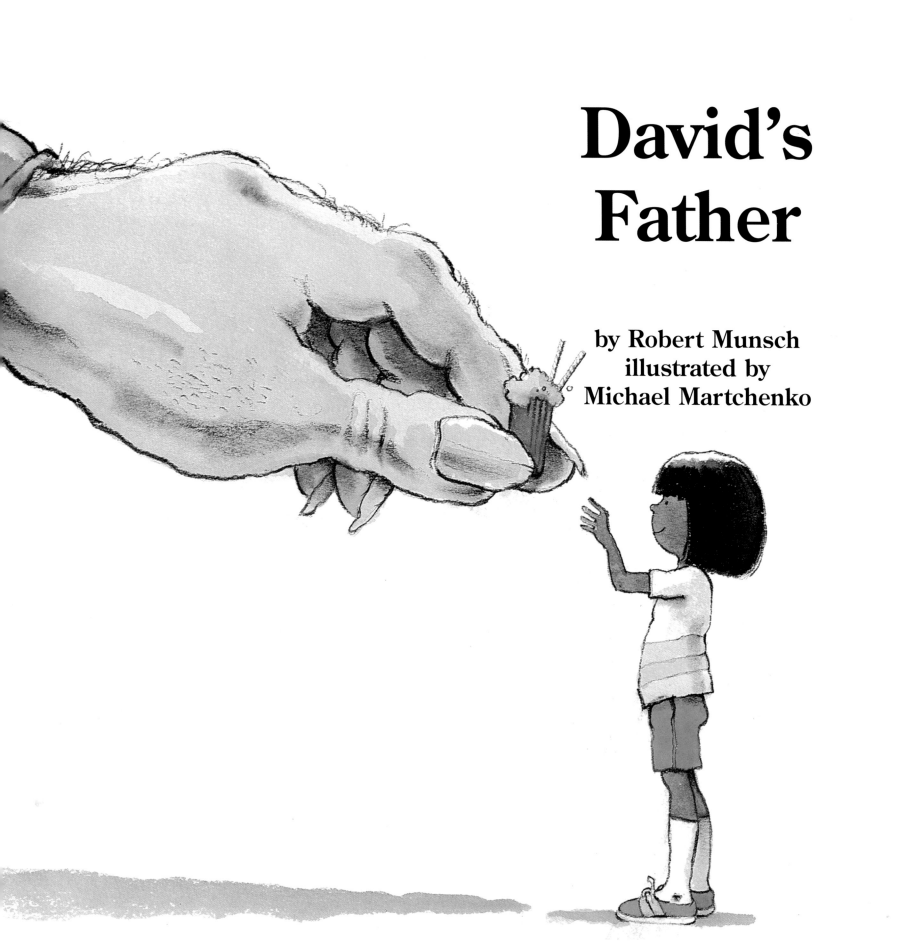

David's Father

by Robert Munsch
illustrated by
Michael Martchenko

*J*ulie was skipping home from school. She came to a large moving van. A man came out carrying a spoon—only it was as big as a shovel. Another man came out carrying a fork—only it was as big as a pitchfork. A third man came out carrying a knife—only it was as big as a flagpole.

"Yikes," said Julie, "I don't want to get to know these people at all."

She ran all the way home and hid under her bed till dinner time.

The next day Julie was skipping home from school again. A boy was standing where the moving van had been. He said, "Hi, my name's David. Would you like to come and play?" Julie looked at him very carefully. He seemed to be a regular sort of boy, so she stayed to play.

At five o'clock, from far away down the street, someone called, "Julie, come and eat."

"That's my mother," said Julie. Then someone called, ***"DAVID!!!"***

"That's my father," said David.

Julie jumped up in the air, ran around in a circle three times, ran home and locked herself in her room till it was time for breakfast the next morning.

The next day Julie was skipping home and she saw David again. He said, "Hi, Julie, do you want to come and play?" Julie looked at him very, very carefully. He seemed to be a regular boy, so she stayed and played.

When it was almost five o'clock, David said, "Julie, please stay for dinner."

But Julie remembered the big knife, the big fork and the big spoon. "Well, I don't know," she said, "maybe it's a bad idea. I think maybe no. Good-bye, good-bye, good-bye."

"Well," said David, "we're having cheese-burgers, chocolate milk shakes and a salad."

"Oh?" said Julie, "I love cheeseburgers. I'll stay, I'll stay."

So they went into the kitchen. There was a small table with cheeseburgers, milk shakes and salads. On the other side of the room there was an enormous table. On it were a spoon as big as a shovel, a fork as big as a pitchfork and a knife as big as a flagpole. "David," whispered Julie, "who sits there?"

"Oh," said David. "That's where my father sits. You can hear him coming now." David's father sounded like this:

broum broum broum

He opened the door.

David's father was a giant. On his table there were 26 snails, three fried octopuses and 16 bricks covered with chocolate sauce.

David and Julie ate their cheeseburgers and the father ate the snails. David and Julie drank their milk shakes and the father ate the fried octopuses. David and Julie ate their salads and the father ate his chocolate-covered bricks.

David's father asked Julie if she would like a snail. Julie said no. David's father asked Julie if she would like an octopus. Julie said no. David's father asked Julie if she would like a delicious chocolate-covered brick. Julie said, "No, but please, may I have another milk shake?" So David's father made her another milk shake.

When they were done Julie said, very softly so the father couldn't hear, "David, you don't look very much like your father."

"Well, I'm adopted," said David.

"Oh," said Julie. "Well, do you like your father?"

"He's great," said David, "come for a walk and see."

So they walked down the street. Julie and David skipped, and the father went

broum broum broum.

They came to a road and they couldn't get across. The cars would not stop for David. The cars would not stop for Julie. The father walked into the middle of the road, looked at the cars and yelled,

"stop."

The cars all jumped up into the air, ran around in a circle three times and went back up the street so fast they forgot their tires.

Julie and David crossed the street and went into a store. The man who ran the store didn't like serving kids. They waited five minutes, 10 minutes, 15 minutes. Then David's father came in. He looked at the storekeeper and said, ***"THESE KIDS ARE MY FRIENDS!"*** The man jumped up into the air, ran around the store three times and gave David and Julie three boxes of ice cream, 11 bags of potato chips and 19 life savers, all for free. Julie and David walked down the street and went around a bend.

There were six big kids from grade eight standing in the middle of the sidewalk. They looked at David. They looked at Julie and they looked at the food. Then one big kid reached down and grabbed a box of ice cream. David's father came round the bend. He looked at the big kids and yelled,

"beat it."

They jumped right out of their shirts. They jumped right out of their pants and ran down the street in their underwear. Julie ran after them, but she slipped and scraped her elbow.

David's father picked her up and held her.
Then he put a special giant bandage on her elbow.
Julie said, "Well, David, you do have a very
nice father after all, but he is still kind of scary."

"You think he is scary?" said David.
"Wait till you meet my grandmother."

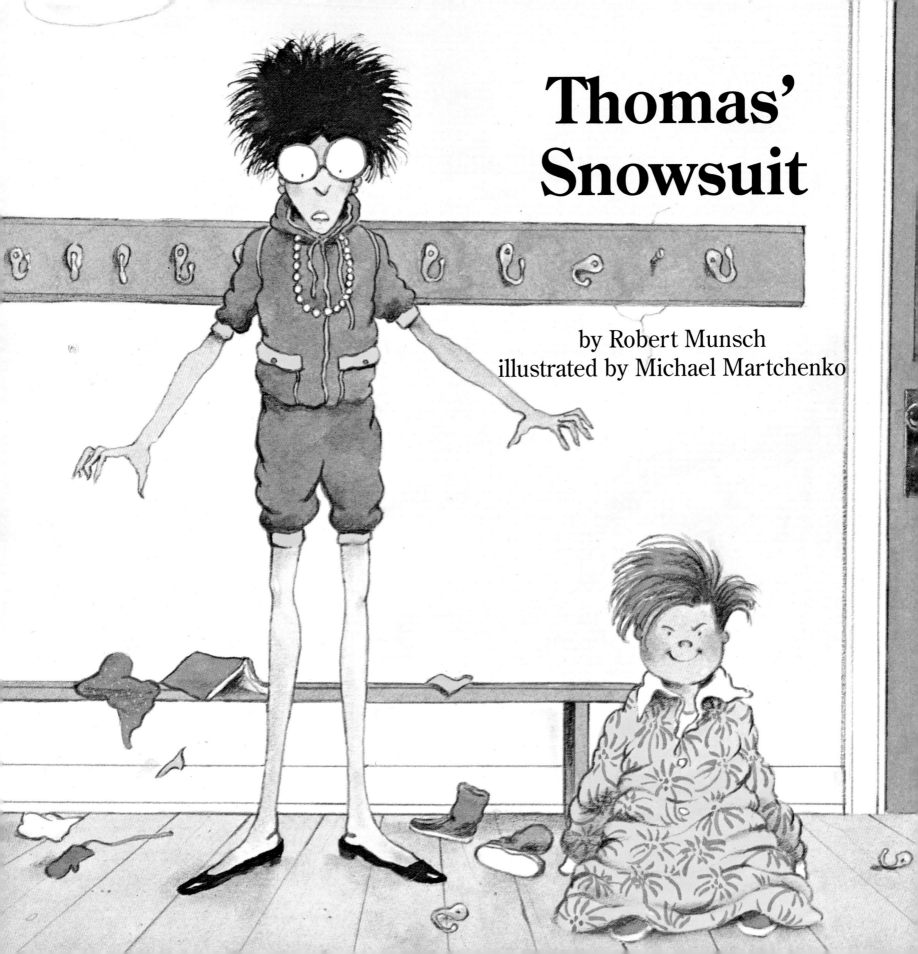

Thomas' Snowsuit

by Robert Munsch
illustrated by Michael Martchenko

*O*ne day, Thomas' mother bought him a nice new brown snowsuit. When Thomas saw that snowsuit he said, "That is the ugliest thing I have ever seen in my life. If you think that I am going to wear that ugly snowsuit, you are crazy!"

Thomas' mother said, "We will see about that."

The next day, when it was time to go to school, the mother said, "Thomas, please put on your snowsuit," and Thomas said, "NNNNNO."

His mother jumped up and down and said,
"Thomas, put on that snowsuit!"

And Thomas said, "NNNNNO!"

So Thomas' mother picked up Thomas in
one hand, picked up the snowsuit in the other
hand, and she tried to stick them together.
They had an enormous fight, and when it was
done Thomas was in his snowsuit.

Thomas went off to school and hung up his snowsuit. When it was time to go outside, all the other kids jumped into their snowsuits and ran out the door. But not Thomas.

The teacher looked at Thomas and said, "Thomas, please put on your snowsuit."

Thomas said, "NNNNNO."

The teacher jumped up and down and said, "Thomas, put on that snowsuit."

And Thomas said, "NNNNNO."

So the teacher picked up Thomas in one hand, picked up the snowsuit in the other hand and she tried to stick them together. They had an enormous fight, and when they were done the teacher was wearing Thomas' snowsuit and Thomas was wearing the teacher's dress.

When the teacher saw what she was wearing, she picked up Thomas in one hand and tried to get him back into his snowsuit. They had an enormous fight. When they were done, the snowsuit and the dress were tied into a great big knot on the floor and Thomas and the teacher were in their underclothes.

Just then the door opened, and in walked the principal. The teacher said, "It's Thomas. He won't put on his snowsuit."

The principal gave his very best
PRINCIPAL LOOK and said, "Thomas, put on
your snowsuit."
And Thomas said, "NNNNNO."

So the principal picked up Thomas in one hand and he picked up the teacher in the other hand, and he tried to get them back into their clothes. When he was done, the principal was wearing the teacher's dress, the teacher was wearing the principal's suit and Thomas was still in his underwear.

Then from far out in the playground some-one yelled, "Thomas, come and play!" Thomas ran across the room, jumped into his snowsuit, got his boots on in two seconds and ran out the door.

The principal looked at the teacher and said, "Hey, you have on my suit. Take it off right now."

The teacher said, "Oh, no. You have on my dress. You take off my dress first."

Well, they argued and argued and argued, but neither one wanted to change first.

Finally, Thomas came in from recess. He looked at the principal and he looked at the teacher. Thomas picked up the principal in one hand. He picked up the teacher in the other hand. They had an enormous fight and Thomas got everybody back into their clothes.

The next day the principal quit his job and moved to Arizona, where nobody ever wears a snowsuit.

Pigs

by Robert Munsch

illustrated by

Michael Martchenko

*M*egan's father asked her to feed the pigs
on her way to school. He said, "Megan, please
feed the pigs, but don't open the gate. Pigs are
smarter than you think. Don't open the gate."

"Right," said Megan. "I will not open the
gate. Not me. No sir. No, no, no, no, no."

So Megan went to the pig pen. She looked at the pigs. The pigs looked at Megan.

Megan said, "These are the dumbest-looking animals I have ever seen. They stand there like lumps on a bump. They wouldn't do anything if I did open the gate." So Megan opened the gate just a little bit. The pigs stood there and looked at Megan. They didn't do anything.

Megan said, "These are the dumbest-looking animals I have ever seen. They stand there like lumps on a bump. They wouldn't even go out the door if the house was on fire." So Megan opened the gate a little bit more. The pigs stood there and looked at Megan. They didn't do anything.

Then Megan yelled, "HEY YOU DUMB PIGS!" The pigs jumped up and ran right over Megan, WAP—WAP—WAP—WAP —WAP, and out the gate.

When Megan got up she couldn't see the pigs anywhere. She said, "Uh-oh, I am in bad trouble. Maybe pigs are not so dumb after all." Then she went to tell her father the bad news. When she got to the house Megan heard a noise coming from the kitchen. It went, "OINK, OINK, OINK."

"That doesn't sound like my mother. That doesn't sound like my father. That sounds like pigs."

She looked in the window. There was her father, sitting at the breakfast table. A pig was drinking his coffee. A pig was eating his newspaper. And a pig was peeing on his shoe.

"Megan," yelled her father, "you opened the gate. Get these pigs out of here."

Megan opened the front door a little bit. The pigs stood and looked at Megan. Finally Megan opened the front door all the way and yelled, "HEY YOU DUMB PIGS!" The pigs jumped up and ran right over Megan, WAP—WAP—WAP—WAP—WAP, and out the door.

Megan ran outside, chased all the pigs into the pig pen and shut the gate. Then she looked at the pigs and said, "You are still dumb, like lumps on a bump." Then she ran off to school. Just as she was about to open the front door, she heard a sound: "OINK, OINK, OINK."

She said, "That doesn't sound like my teacher. That doesn't sound like the principal. That sounds like pigs."

Megan looked in the principal's window. There was a pig drinking the principal's coffee. A pig was eating the principal's newspaper. And a pig was peeing on the principal's shoe. The principal yelled, "Megan, get these pigs out of here!"

Megan opened the front door of the school a little bit. The pigs didn't do anything. She opened the door a little bit more. The pigs still didn't do anything. She opened the door all the way and yelled, "HEY YOU DUMB PIGS!" The pigs jumped up and ran right over Megan, WAP—WAP—WAP—WAP—WAP, and out the door.

Megan went into the school. She sat down at her desk and said, "That's that! I finally got rid of all the pigs." Then she heard a noise: "OINK, OINK, OINK." Megan opened her desk, and there was a new baby pig. The teacher said, "Megan! Get that dumb pig out of here!"

Megan said, "Dumb? Who ever said pigs were dumb? Pigs are smart. I am going to keep it for a pet."

At the end of the day the school bus finally came. Megan walked up to the door, then heard something say, "OINK, OINK, OINK."

Megan said, "That doesn't sound like the bus driver. That sounds like a pig." She climbed up the stairs and looked in the bus. There was a pig driving the bus, pigs eating the seats and pigs lying in the aisle.

A pig shut the door and drove the bus down the road.

It drove the bus all the way to Megan's farm, through the barnyard and right into the pig pen.

Megan got out of the bus, walked across the barnyard and marched into the kitchen. She said, "The pigs are all back in the pig pen. They came back by themselves. Pigs are smarter than you think."

And Megan never let out any more animals.

At least, not any more pigs.

Mortimer

by Robert Munsch
illustrated by
Michael Martchenko

*O*ne night Mortimer's mother took him upstairs to go to bed—

thump thump thump thump thump thump.

When they got upstairs Mortimer's mother opened the door to his room.

She threw him into bed and said,

"MORTIMER, BE QUIET."

Mortimer shook his head, yes.

The mother shut the door.
Then she went back down the stairs—
thump
 thump
  thump
   thump
    thump.

As soon as she got back downstairs
Mortimer sang,

Clang, clang, rattle-bing-bang
Gonna make my noise all day.
Clang, clang, rattle-bing-bang
Gonna make my noise all day.

Mortimer's father heard all that noise.
He came up the stairs—

thump thump thump thump thump^{thump} thump.

He opened the door and yelled,

"MORTIMER, BE QUIET."

Mortimer shook his head, yes.

The father went back down the stairs—
thump thump thump thump thump thump.

As soon as he got to the bottom of the stairs Mortimer sang,

Clang, clang, rattle-bing-bang
Gonna make my noise all day.
Clang, clang, rattle-bing-bang
Gonna make my noise all day.

All of Mortimer's seventeen brothers and sisters heard that noise, and they all came up the stairs—

thump
thump
thump
thump
thump
thump.

They opened the door and yelled in a tremendous, loud voice,

"MORTIMER, BE QUIET."

Mortimer shook his head, yes.

The brothers and sisters shut the door
and went downstairs—
thump
 thump
  thump
   thump
    thump.

As soon as they got to the bottom of the
stairs Mortimer sang,

    Clang, clang, rattle-bing-bang
    Gonna make my noise all day.
    Clang, clang, rattle-bing-bang
    Gonna make my noise all day.

They got so upset that they called the police. Two policemen came and they walked very slowly up the stairs—

thump.

thump

thump

thump

thump

thump

thump

They opened the door and said in very deep, policemen-type voices,

"MORTIMER, BE QUIET."

The policemen shut the door and went
back down the stairs—
thump
  thump
    thump
      thump
        thump.

As soon as they got to the bottom of the
stairs Mortimer sang,

> Clang, clang, rattle-bing-bang
> Gonna make my noise all day.
> Clang, clang, rattle-bing-bang
> Gonna make my noise all day.

Well, downstairs no one knew what to do.
The mother got into a big fight with the
policemen.
The father got into a big fight with the
brothers and sisters.

Upstairs, Mortimer got so tired waiting for someone to come up that he fell asleep.

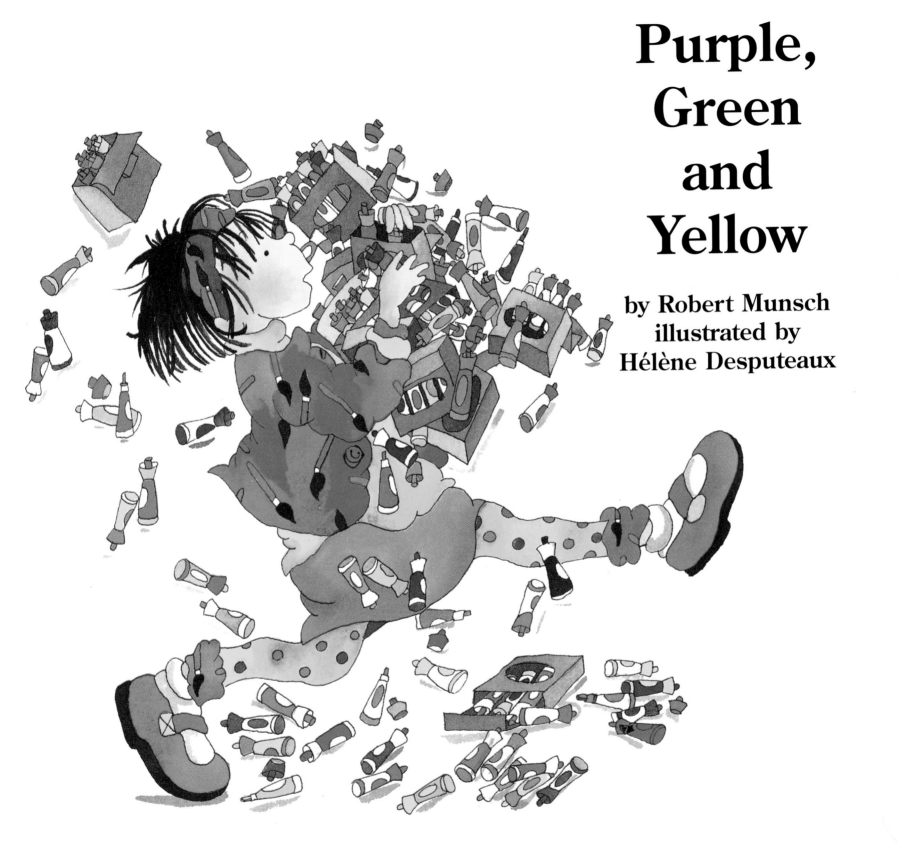

Purple,
Green
and
Yellow

by Robert Munsch
illustrated by
Hélène Desputeaux

*B*rigid went to her mother and said, "I need some coloring markers. All my friends have coloring markers. They draw wonderful pictures. Mommy, I need some coloring markers."

"Oh, no!" said her mother. "I've heard about those coloring markers. Kids draw on walls, they draw on the floor, they draw on them-selves. You can't have any coloring markers."

"Well," said Brigid, "there are these new coloring markers. They wash off with just water. I can't get into any trouble with coloring markers that wash off. Get me some of those."

"Well," said her mother, "all right."

So her mother went out and got Brigid 500 washable coloring markers.

Brigid went up to her room and drew wonderful pictures. She drew lemons that were yellower than lemons, and roses that were redder than roses, and oranges that were oranger than oranges.

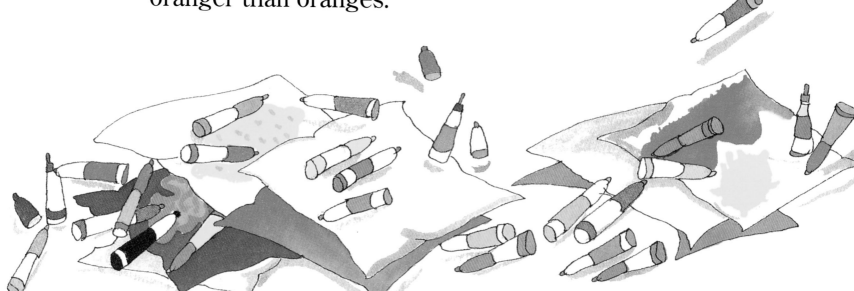

Her mother was amazed. She said,
"Wow! My kid is an artist."

But after a week Brigid got bored. She went to her mother and said, "Mom, did I draw on the wall?"

"Nnnnooo," said her mother.

"Did I draw on the floor?"

"Nnnnooo," said her mother.

"Did I draw on myself?"

"Nnnnooo," said her mother.

"Well," said Brigid, "I didn't get into any trouble and I need some new coloring markers. All my friends have them. Mommy, there are coloring markers that smell. They have ones that smell like roses and lemons and oranges and even ones that smell like cow plops. Mom, they have coloring markers that smell like anything you want! Mom, I need those coloring markers."

Her mother went out and got 500 coloring markers that smelled. Then Brigid went upstairs and she drew pictures. She drew lemons that smelled like lemons, and roses that smelled like roses, and oranges that smelled like oranges, and cow plops that smelled like cow plops.

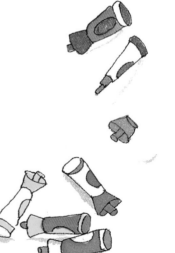

Her mother said, "Wow! My kid is an artist."

184

But after a week Brigid got bored. She said, "Mom, did I draw on the floor?"

"Nnnnooo," said her mother.

"Did I draw on the walls?"

"Nnnnooo," said her mother.

"Did I draw on myself?"

"Nnnnooo," said her mother.

"Well," said Brigid, "I need some new coloring markers. These are the best kind. All my friends have them. They are super-indelible-never-come-off-till-you're-dead-and-maybe-even-later coloring markers. Mom, I need them."

So her mother went out and got 500 super-indelible-never-come-off-till-you're-dead-and-maybe-even-later coloring markers. Brigid took them and drew pictures for three weeks. She drew lemons that looked better than lemons, and roses that looked better than roses and oranges that looked better than oranges and sunsets that looked better than sunsets.

Then she got bored.

She said, "I'm tired of drawing on the paper. But I am not going to draw on the walls and I am not going to draw on the floor and I'm not going to draw on myself —but everybody knows it's okay to color your fingernails. Even my mother colors her fingernails."

So Brigid took a purple super-indelible-never-come-off-till-you're-dead-and-maybe-even-later coloring marker, and she colored her thumbnail bright purple.

And that was so pretty, she colored all her fingernails purple, black and yellow.

And that was so pretty, she colored her hands yellow, green and red.

And that was so pretty, she colored her face purple, green, yellow and blue.

And that was so pretty, she colored her belly-button blue.

190

And that was so pretty, she colored herself all sorts of colors almost entirely all over.

Then Brigid looked in the mirror and said, "What have I done! My mother is going to kill me." So she ran into the bathroom and washed her hands for half an hour. Nothing came off. Her hands still looked like mixed-up rainbows.

Then she had a wonderful idea.

She reached way down into the bottom of the coloring markers and got a special-colored marker. It was the same color she was. She took that marker and colored herself all over until she was her regular color again. In fact, she looked even better than before—almost too good to be true.

She went downstairs and her mother said, "Why, Brigid, you're looking really good today."

"Right," said Brigid.

Then her mother said, "It's time to wash your hands for dinner."

But Brigid was afraid that the special color would not stick to the colors underneath, so she said, "I already washed my hands."

But her mother smelled her hands and said, "Ahhh. No soap!" She took Brigid into the bathroom and washed her hands and face. All the special color came off and Brigid looked like mixed-up rainbows.

"Oh, no!" said her mother. "Brigid, did you color your hands with the coloring markers that wash off?"

"Nnnnooo."

"Brigid, did you color your hands with the coloring markers that smell?"

"Nnnnnooooo."

"Did you use the super-indelible-never-come-off-till-you're-dead-and-maybe-even-later coloring markers?"

"Yes!"

"Yikes!" yelled her mother.

She called the doctor and said, "HELP! HELP! HELP! My daughter has colored herself with super-indelible-never-come-off-till-you're-dead-and-maybe-even-later coloring markers."

"Oh, dear," said the doctor. "Sometimes they never come off."

The doctor came over and gave Brigid a large, orange pill. She said, "Take this pill, wait five minutes and then take a bath."

So Brigid took the pill, waited five minutes, and jumped into the bathtub. Her mother stood outside the door and yelled, "Is it working? Is it working?"

"Yes," said Brigid. "Everything is coming off." And Brigid was right, everything had come off. When Brigid walked out of the bathroom she was invisible.

"Oh, no," yelled her mother. "You can't go to school if you're invisible. You can't go to university if you're invisible. You'll never get a job if you're invisible. Brigid, you've wrecked your life!"

"Don't worry," said Brigid. She ran into her room, got the special-colored marker and colored herself entirely all over until you couldn't tell the difference. In fact, she looked even better than before — almost too good to be true.

But her mother said, "Brigid, you can't go through life like that. You're just a picture. Everyone will know there is something wrong."

"No they won't," said Brigid.

"Yes they will," said her mother.

"No they won't," said Brigid. "I colored Daddy while he was taking a nap and you haven't noticed anything yet!"

"Good heavens!" yelled her mother, and she ran into the living-room and looked at Daddy. He looked even better than before—almost too good to be true.

"Doesn't he look great?" asked Brigid.

"I couldn't even tell the difference," said her mother.

"Right," said Brigid, "and neither will he...

As long as he doesn't get wet."

Murmel, Murmel, Murmel

by Robert Munsch
illustrated by
Michael Martchenko

When Robin went out into her back yard, there was a large hole right in the middle of her sandbox. She knelt down beside it and yelled, "ANYBODY DOWN THERE?"

From way down the hole something said, "Murmel, murmel, murmel."

"Hmmm," said Robin, "very strange." So she yelled, even louder, "ANYBODY DOWN THERE?"

"Murmel, murmel, murmel," said the hole. Robin reached down the hole as far as she could and gave an enormous yank. Out popped a baby.

"Murmel, murmel, murmel," said the baby.

"Murmel, yourself," said Robin. "I am only five years old and I can't take care of a baby. I will find somebody else to take care of you."

Robin picked up the very heavy baby and walked down the street. She met a woman pushing a baby carriage. Robin said, "Excuse me, do you need a baby?"

"Heavens, no," said the woman. "I already have a baby." She went off down the street and seventeen diaper salesmen jumped out from behind a hedge and ran after her.

Robin picked up the baby and went on down the street. She met an old woman and said, "Excuse me, do you need a baby?"

"Does it pee its pants?" said the old lady.

"Yes," said Robin.

"Yecch," said the old lady. "Does it dirty its diaper?"

"Yes," said Robin.

"Yecch," said the old lady. "Does it have a runny nose?"

"Yes," said Robin.

"Yecch," said the old lady. "I already have seventeen cats. I don't need a baby." She went off down the street. Seventeen cats jumped out of a garbage can and ran after her.

Robin picked up the baby and went down the street. She met a woman in fancy clothes. "Excuse me," said Robin, "do you need a baby?"

"Heavens, no," said the woman. "I have seventeen jobs, lots of money and no time. I don't need a baby." She went off down the street. Seventeen secretaries, nine messengers and a pizza delivery man ran after her.

"Rats," said Robin. She picked up the baby and walked down the street. She met a man. "Excuse me," she said, "do you need a baby?"

"I don't know," said the man. "Can it wash my car?"

"No," said Robin.

"Can I sell it for lots of money?"

"No," said Robin.

"Well, what is it for?" said the man.

"It is for loving and hugging and feeding and burping," said Robin.

"I certainly don't need that," said the man. He went off down the street. Nobody followed him.

Robin sat down beside the street, for the baby was getting very heavy.

"Murmel, murmel, murmel," said the baby.

"Murmel, yourself," said Robin. "What am I going to do with you?"

An enormous truck came by and stopped.

A truck driver jumped out and walked around Robin three times. Then he looked at the baby.

"Excuse me," said Robin, "do you need a baby?"

The truck driver said, "Weeeellll..."

"Murmel, murmel, murmel," said the baby.

"Did you say, 'murmel, murmel, murmel'?"asked the truck driver.

"Yes!" said the baby.

"I need you," yelled the truck driver. He picked up the baby and started walking down the street.

"Wait," said Robin, "you forgot your truck!"

"I already have seventeen trucks," said the truck driver. "What I need is a baby..."

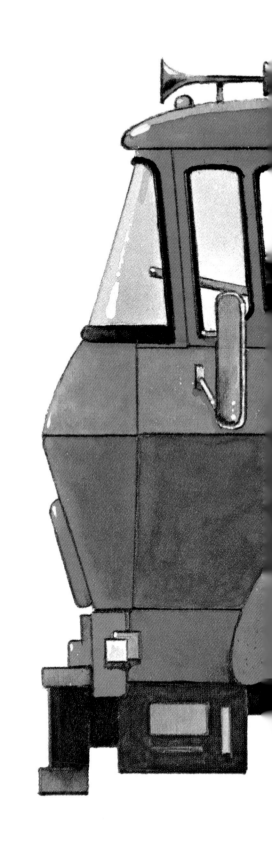

"YOU can have the truck."

Something Good

by Robert Munsch
illustrated by
Michael Martchenko

Tyya went shopping with her father and her brother and her sister. She pushed the cart up the aisle and down the aisle, up the aisle and down the aisle, up the aisle and down the aisle.

Tyya said, "Sometimes my father doesn't buy good food. He gets bread, eggs, milk, cheese, spinach—nothing any good! He doesn't buy ICE CREAM! COOKIES! CHOCOLATE BARS! or GINGER ALE!"

So Tyya very quietly snuck away from her father and got a cart of her own. She pushed it over to the ice cream. Then she put one hundred boxes of ice cream into her cart.

Tyya pushed that cart up behind her father and said, "DADDY, LOOK!" Her father turned around and yelled, "YIKES!"

Tyya said, "DADDY! GOOD FOOD!"

"Oh, no," said her father. "This is sugary junk. It will rot your teeth. It will lower your IQ. Put it ALL BACK!"

So Tyya put back the one hundred boxes of ice cream. She meant to go right back to her father, but on the way she had to pass the candy. She put three hundred chocolate bars into her cart.

Tyya pushed that cart up behind her father and said, "DADDY, LOOK!" Her father turned around and said, "YIKES!"

Tyya said, "DADDY! GOOD FOOD!"

"Oh, no," said her father. "This is sugary junk. Put it ALL BACK!" So Tyya put back all the chocolate bars. Then her father said, "Okay, Tyya, I have had it. You stand here and DON'T MOVE."

Tyya knew she was in BIG trouble, so she stood there and DIDN'T MOVE. Some friends came by and said hello. Tyya didn't move. A man ran over her toe with his cart. Tyya still didn't move.

A lady who worked at the store came by and looked at Tyya. She looked her over from the top down, and she looked her over from the bottom up. She knocked Tyya on the head—and Tyya still didn't move.

The lady said, "This is the nicest doll I have ever seen. It looks almost real." She put a price tag on Tyya's nose that said $29.95. Then she picked Tyya up and put her on the shelf with all the other dolls.

A man came along and looked at Tyya. He said, "This is the nicest doll I have ever seen. I'm going to get that doll for my son." He picked up Tyya by the hair.

Tyya yelled, very loudly, "STOP."

The man screamed, "EYAAAAH! IT'S ALIVE!" And he ran down the aisle, knocking over a pile of five hundred apples.

A lady came along and looked at Tyya. She said, "This is the nicest doll I have ever seen. I think I will buy this doll for my daughter." She picked up Tyya by the ear. Tyya yelled, as loudly as she could, "STOP."

The lady screamed, "EYAAAAH! IT'S ALIVE!" And she ran down the aisle, knocking over a pile of five hundred oranges.

Then Tyya's father came along, looking for his daughter. He said, "Tyya? Tyya? Tyya? Tyya? Where are you? ... TYYA! What are you doing on that shelf?"

Tyya said, "It's all your fault. You told me not to move and people are trying to buy me, WAAAAAHHHHH!"

"Oh, come now," said her father. "I won't let anybody buy you." He gave Tyya a big kiss and a big hug; then they went to pay for all the food.

The man at the cash register looked at Tyya and said, "Hey, Mister, you can't take that kid out of the store. You have to pay for her. It says so right on her nose: twenty-nine ninety-five."

"Wait," said the father. "This is my own kid. I don't have to pay for my own kid."

The man said, "If it has a price tag, you have to pay for it."

"I won't pay," said the father.

"You've got to," said the man.

The father said, "NNNNO."

The man said, "YYYYES."

The father said, "NNNNO!"

The man said, "YYYYES!"

The father and Andrew and Julie all yelled, "NNNNNNO!"

Then Tyya quietly said, "Daddy, don't you think I'm worth twenty-nine ninety-five?"

"Ah...Um...I mean... Well, of course you're worth twenty-nine ninety-five," said the father. He reached into his wallet, got out the money, paid the man, and took the price tag off Tyya's nose.

Tyya gave her father a big kiss, SMMMER-CCHH, and a big hug, MMMMMMMMMM, and then she said, "Daddy, you finally bought something good after all."

Then her father picked up Tyya and gave her a big long hug—and didn't say anything at all.

Stephanie's Ponytail

by Robert Munsch
illustrated by
Michael Martchenko

*O*ne day Stephanie went to her mom and said, "None of the kids in my class have a ponytail. I want a nice ponytail coming right out the back."

So Stephanie's mom gave her a nice ponytail coming right out the back.

When Stephanie went to school, the other kids looked at her and said, "Ugly, ugly, very ugly."

Stephanie said, "It's *my ponytail* and *I* like it."

The next morning, when Stephanie went to school, all the other girls had ponytails coming out the back.

Stephanie looked at them and said, "You are all a bunch of copycats. You just do whatever I do. You don't have a brain in your heads."

The next morning the mom said, "Stephanie, would you like a ponytail coming out the back?"

Stephanie said, "No."

"Then that's that," said her mom. "That's the only place you can do ponytails."

"No, it's not," said Stephanie. "I want one coming out the side, just above my ear."

"Very strange," said the mom. "Are you sure that is what you want?"

"Yes," said Stephanie.

So her mom gave Stephanie a nice ponytail coming out right above her ear.

When she went to school, the other kids saw her and said, "Ugly, ugly, very ugly."

Stephanie said, "It's *my ponytail* and *I* like it."

The next morning, when Stephanie came to school, all the girls, and even some of the boys, had nice ponytails coming out just above their ears.

The next morning the mom said, "Stephanie, would you like a ponytail coming out the back?"

Stephanie said, "NNNO."

"Would you like one coming out the side?"

"NNNO!"

"Then that's that," said her mom. "There is no other place you can do ponytails."

"Yes, there is," said Stephanie. "I want one coming out of the top of my head like a tree."

"That's very, very strange," said her mom. "Are you sure that is what you want?"

"Yes," said Stephanie.

So her mom gave Stephanie a nice ponytail coming out of the top of her head like a tree. When Stephanie went to school, the other kids saw her and said, "Ugly, ugly, very ugly."

Stephanie said, "It's *my ponytail* and *I* like it."

The next day all of the girls and all of the boys had ponytails coming out the top. It looked like broccoli was growing out of their heads.

The next morning the mom said, "Stephanie, would you like a ponytail coming out the back?"

Stephanie said, "NNNO."

"Would you like one coming out the side?"

"NNNO!"

"Would you like one coming out the top?"

"*NNNO!*"

"Then that is definitely that," said the mom. "There is no other place you can do ponytails."

"Yes, there is," said Stephanie. "I want one coming out the front and hanging down in front of my nose."

"But nobody will know if you are coming or going," her mom said. "Are you sure that is what you want?"

"Yes," said Stephanie. So her mom gave Stephanie a nice ponytail coming out the front.

On the way to school she bumped into four trees, three cars, two houses and one Principal.

When she finally got to her class, the other kids saw her and said, "Ugly, ugly, very ugly."

Stephanie said, "It's *my ponytail* and *I* like it."

The next day all of the girls and all of the boys, and even the teacher, had ponytails coming out the front and hanging down in front of their noses. None of them could see where they were going. They bumped into the desks and they bumped into each other. They bumped into the walls and, by mistake, three girls went into the boys' bathroom.

Stephanie yelled, "You are a bunch of brainless copycats. You just do whatever I do. When I come tomorrow, I am going to have ... SHAVED MY HEAD!"

The first person to come the next day was the teacher. She had shaved her head and she was bald.

The next to come were the boys. They had shaved their heads and they were bald.

The next to come were the girls. They had shaved their heads and they were bald.

The last person to come was Stephanie, and she had ...

a nice little ponytail coming right out the back.

Angela's Airplane

by Robert Munsch
illustrated by
Michael Martchenko

*A*ngela's father took her to the airport, but when they got there, a terrible thing happened: Angela's father got lost.

Angela looked under airplanes and on top of airplanes and beside airplanes, but she couldn't find him anyplace, so Angela decided to look *inside* an airplane.

She saw one with an open door and climbed up the steps: one, two, three, four, five, six—right to the top. Her father was not there, and neither was anyone else.

Angela had never been in an airplane before. In the front there was a seat that had lots of buttons all around it. Angela loved to push buttons, so she walked up to the front, sat down in the seat and said to herself, "It's okay if I push just *one* button. Don't you think it's okay if I push just *one* button? Oh yes, it's okay. Yes, yes, yes, yes."

Then she slowly pressed the bright red button. Right away the door closed.

Angela said, "It's okay if I push just one more button. Don't you think it's okay if I push just one more button? Oh yes, it's okay. Yes, yes, yes, yes." Slowly she pushed the yellow button. Right away the lights came on.

Angela said, "It's okay if I push just *one more* button. Don't you think it's okay if I push just *one more* button? Oh yes, it's okay. Yes, yes, yes, yes." She pushed the green button. Right away the motor came on: VROOM, VROOM, VROOM, VROOM.

Angela said, "Yikes," and pushed all the buttons at once. The airplane took off and went right up into the air.

When Angela looked out the window, she saw that she was very high in the sky. She didn't know how to get down. The only thing to do was to push one more button, so she slowly pushed the black button. It was the radio button. A voice came on the radio and said, "Bring back that airplane, you thief, you."

Angela said, "My name is Angela. I am five years old and I don't know how to fly airplanes."

"Oh dear," said the voice. "What a mess. Listen carefully, Angela. Take the steering wheel and turn it to the left."

Angela turned the wheel and very slowly
the airplane went in a big circle and came back
right over the airport.

"Okay," said the voice, "now pull back on
the wheel."

Angela pulled back on the wheel and the airplane slowly went down to the runway. It hit once and bounced. It hit again and bounced. Then one wing scraped the ground. Right away the whole plane smashed and broke into little pieces.

Angela was left sitting on the ground and she didn't even have a scratch.

All sorts of cars and trucks came speeding out of the terminal.

There were police cars, ambulances, fire trucks and buses. And all sorts of people came running, but in front of everybody was Angela's father.

He picked her up and said, "Angela, are you all right?"

"Yes," said Angela.

"Oh, Angela," he said, "the airplane is not all right. It is in very small pieces."

"I know," said Angela, "it was a mistake."

"Well, Angela," said her father, "promise me you will never fly another airplane."

"I promise," said Angela.

"Are you sure?" said the father.

Angela said, very loudly, "I promise, I promise, I promise."

Angela didn't fly an airplane for a very long time. But when she grew up, she didn't become a doctor, she didn't become a truck driver, she didn't become a secretary and she didn't become a nurse. She became an airplane pilot.

Jonathan Cleaned Up—Then He Heard a Sound

by Robert Munsch

illustrated by Michael Martchenko

*J*onathan's mother went to get a can of noodles. She said, "Jonathan, please don't make a mess!"

When she was gone, Jonathan stood in the middle of the apartment and looked at the nice clean rug and the nice clean walls and the very, very clean sofa and said, "Well, there is certainly no mess here."

Then he heard a sound. It was coming from behind the wall. He put his ear up against the wall and listened very carefully.

The noise sounded like a train. Just then, the
wall slid open and a subway train pulled up
and stopped. Someone yelled, "LAST STOP!
EVERYBODY OUT!" Then little people, big
people, fat people and thin people, and all
kinds of people, came out of Jonathan's wall,
ran around his apartment and went out the
front door.

Jonathan stood in the middle of the living room and looked around. There was writing on the wall, gum on the rug and a man sleeping on the sofa, and all the food was gone from the refrigerator.

"Well," said Jonathan, "this is certainly a mess!" Jonathan tried to drag the man out the door, but he met his mother coming in.

She saw the writing on the wall, the gum on the rug and the empty refrigerator. She yelled, "Jonathan, what a mess!"

Jonathan said, "The wall opened up and there was a subway train. Thousands of people came running through."

But his mother said, "Oh, Jon, don't be silly. Clean it up."

She went out to get another can of noodles, and Jonathan cleaned up. When he was all done, he heard a sound. It was coming from behind the wall. He put his ear up against the wall and listened very carefully. The noise sounded like a train. Someone yelled, "LAST STOP! EVERYBODY OUT!" And all kinds of people came out of Jonathan's wall, ran around his apartment and went out the front door.

This time there were ice cream cones and chewing gum on the rug, writing and foot-prints on the wall, two men sleeping on the sofa and a policeman watching TV. Besides that, the refrigerator was gone. Jonathan got angry and yelled, "Everybody out."

Just then his mother came in. She saw ice cream cones and chewing gum on the rug, writing and footprints on the wall, two men sleeping on the sofa, a policeman watching TV and a big empty space where the refrigerator had been. "Jonathan," she said, "what have you done?"

Then she heard a noise. It was coming from behind the wall. She put her ear right against the wall and listened very carefully. The noise sounded like a train. Just then the wall slid open and a subway train pulled up. Someone yelled, "LAST STOP! EVERYBODY OUT!" And all kinds of people ran out of Jonathan's wall, ran around his apartment and went out the front door.

There were ice cream cones, chewing gum and pretzel bags on the rug, writing and footprints and handprints on the wall, and five men sleeping on the sofa. Besides that, a policeman and a conductor were watching TV, and the fridge and stove were gone.

Jonathan went to the conductor and said, "This is not a subway station, this is my house!"

The conductor said, "If the subway stops here, then it's a subway station! You shouldn't build your house in a subway station. If you don't like it, go see City Hall."

So Jonathan went to City Hall.

When he got there, the lady at the front desk told him to see the subway boss, and the subway boss told Jonathan to go see the Mayor.

So he went and saw the Mayor. The Mayor said, "If the subway stops there, then it's a subway station! You shouldn't build your house in a subway station. Our computer says it's a subway station, and our computer is never wrong." Then he ran out for lunch.

In fact, everyone ran out for lunch, and
Jonathan was all by himself at City Hall.
Jonathan started to leave, but on his way out
he heard a sound.

Someone was crying, "Oooooooh, I'm hungry."
Jonathan listened very carefully. He walked up
and down the hall and found the room it was
coming from. He went in, and there was a big,
enormous, shining computer machine. The
computer was going "wing, wing, kler-klung,
clickety clang," and its lights were going off and
on. The voice was coming from behind it.

Jonathan squeezed in back of the machine and saw a little old man at a very messy desk. The man looked at Jonathan and said, "Do you have any blackberry jam?"

"No," said Jonathan, "but I could get you some. Who are you?"

"I'm the computer," said the man.

Now, Jonathan was no dummy. He said, "Computers are machines, and you are not a machine. They go 'wing, wing, kler-klung, clickety clang.'"

The man pointed at the big computer and said, "Well, that goes 'wing, wing, kler-klung, clickety clang,' but the darn thing never did work. I do everything for the whole city."

"Oh," said Jonathan. "I will get you some blackberry jam if you'll do me a favor. A subway station is in my house at 980 Young Street. Please change it."

"Certainly," said the old man. "I remember doing that. I didn't know where to put it."

Jonathan ran out and passed all the offices with nobody there. He ran down the stairs and all the way to a jam store. He got four cases of jam. It took him three hours to carry it all the way back to City Hall. There was still nobody there. He carried the jam back behind the computer and put it on the floor.

"Now," said the old man, "where am I going to put this subway station?"

"I know," said Jonathan, and he whispered in the old man's ear. Then he left. But the old man yelled after him, "Don't tell anyone the computer is broken. The Mayor would be very upset. He paid ten million dollars for it."

When Jonathan got home, his mother was still standing on the rug, because she was stuck to the gum.

Jonathan started washing the writing off the wall. He said, "There will be no more subways here."

And he was right.

Show and Tell

by Robert Munsch
illustrated by
Michael Martchenko

Benjamin wanted to take something really neat to school for show and tell, so he decided to take his new baby sister. He went upstairs, picked her up, put her in his knapsack and walked off to school.

But when Ben sat down, his baby sister finally woke up. She was not happy inside the knapsack and started to cry: "WAAA, WAAA, WAAA, WAAA, WAAA."

The teacher looked at him and said, "Benjamin, stop making that noise."

Ben said, "That's not me. It's my baby sister. She's in my knapsack. I brought her for show and tell."

"Yikes!" said the teacher. "You can't keep a baby in a knapsack!" She grabbed Ben's knapsack and opened it up. The baby looked at the teacher and said, "WAAA, WAAA, WAAA, WAAA, WAAA."

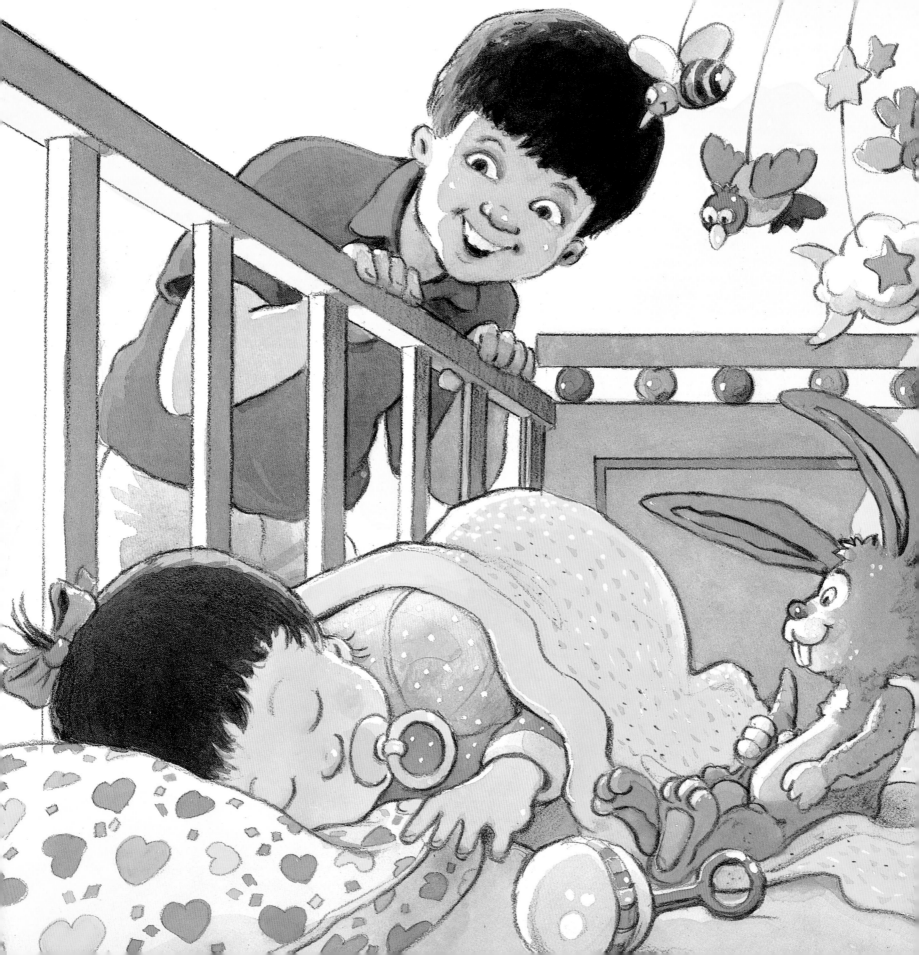

But when Ben sat down, his baby sister finally woke up. She was not happy inside the knapsack and started to cry: "WAAA, WAAA, WAAA, WAAA, WAAA."

The teacher looked at him and said, "Benjamin, stop making that noise."

Ben said, "That's not me. It's my baby sister. She's in my knapsack. I brought her for show and tell."

"Yikes!" said the teacher. "You can't keep a baby in a knapsack!" She grabbed Ben's knapsack and opened it up. The baby looked at the teacher and said, "WAAA, WAAA, WAAA, WAAA, WAAA."

"Don't worry," said the teacher. "I know how to take care of babies." She picked it up and rocked it back and forth, back and forth, back and forth.

Unfortunately, the teacher was not the baby's mother and she didn't rock quite right. The baby cried even louder: "WAAA, WAAA, WAAA, WAAA, WAAA."

The principal came running in. He looked at the teacher and said, "Stop making that noise!"

The teacher said, "It's not me. It's Sharon, Ben's new baby sister. He brought her for show and tell. She won't shut up!"

The principal said, "Ah, don't worry. I know how to make kids be quiet." He picked up the baby and yelled, "HEY, YOU! BE QUIET!" The baby did not like that at all. It screamed, really loudly, "WAAA, WAAA, WAAA, WAAA, WAAA."

The principal said, "What's the matter with this baby? It must be sick. I'll call a doctor."

The doctor came with a big black bag. She looked in the baby's eyes and she looked in the baby's ears and she looked in the baby's mouth. She said, "Ah! Don't worry. I know what to do. This baby needs a needle!"

So the doctor opened her bag, got out a short needle and said, "Naaaah, TOO SMALL."

The doctor opened her bag, got out a longer needle and said, "Naaaah, TOO SMALL."

The doctor opened her bag, got out a really long needle and said, "Naaaah, TOO SMALL."

The doctor reached into her bag, got out an enormous needle and said, "Ahhh, JUST RIGHT."

When the baby saw that enormous needle, it yelled, as loudly as it could, "WAAA, WAAA, WAAA, WAAA, WAAA."

Ben said, "What's the matter with this school? Nobody knows what to do with a baby." He ran down to the principal's office and called his mother on the phone. He said, "HELP, HELP, HELP! You have to come to school right away."

The mother said, "Ben, your little sister is lost! I can't come to school. I have to find her."

"She's not lost," said Ben. "I took her to school in my knapsack."

"Oh, no!" yelled the mother. She ran down the street and into the school. The principal and the teacher and the doctor were standing around the baby, and the baby was yelling, as loudly as possible, "WAAA, WAAA, WAAA, WAAA, WAAA."

The mother picked up the baby
and rocked it back and forth,
back and forth, back and forth.
The baby said, "Ahhhhhhhhh,"
and went to sleep.

344

"Oh, thank you! Oh, thank you!" said the principal. "That baby was making so much noise, it was just making me feel sick!"

"SICK?" said the doctor. "SICK! Did that man say he was SICK? He must need a needle." So the doctor opened her bag, got out a short needle and said, "Naaaah, TOO SMALL."

The doctor opened her bag, got out a longer needle and said, "Naaaah, TOO SMALL."

The doctor opened her bag, got out a really long needle and said, "Naaaah, TOO SMALL."

The doctor reached into her bag, got out an enormous needle and said, "Ahhh, JUST RIGHT."

The principal looked at that enormous needle and said, "WAAA, WAAA, WAAA, WAAA, WAAA," and ran out the door.

"Now," said the mother, "it's time to take this baby home."

"Right," said Ben. "You can use my knapsack."

"What a good idea," said the mother.

Ben and his mother put the baby into bed.
She went to sleep and didn't cry, not even once.

Ben went back to school carrying some strange things for show and tell.

And he wasn't out of place at all ...

A Promise is a Promise

by Robert Munsch and Michael Kusugak
illustrated by Vladyana Krykorka

*O*n the very first nice day of spring Allashua said, "I'm going to go fishing. I'm going to go fishing in the ocean. I'm going to go fishing in the cracks in the ice."

"Ah, ah," said her mother, "don't go fishing on the sea ice. Under the sea ice live Qallupilluit. They grab children who aren't with their parents. Don't go fishing in the ocean. Go fish in a lake."

"Right," said Allashua. "I promise to go fishing in the lake and not in the ocean, and a promise is a promise."

So Allashua set out like she was going to go to the lake near her house, but when she got to the end of the street, she didn't go to the lake. She walked down the long snowy path that led to the ocean.

At the edge of the ocean were large cracks where the tide broke and jumbled the ice. Allashua looked very carefully and did not see any Qallupilluit. She said, "On TV I have seen Santa Claus, Fairy Godmothers and the Tooth Fairy, but never any Qallupilluit. I think my mother is wrong."

But just in case her mother was right, Allashua stood beside the sea ice and yelled, "Qallupilluit have dirty noses."

Nothing happened.

Allashua yelled, "Qallupilluit smell like a dead whale in the summer."

Nothing happened.

Allashua walked right out onto the sea ice and yelled, as loud as she could, "Qallupilluit, Qallupilluit can't catch me!"

Nothing happened. The only thing Allashua heard was the sound of snow blowing over the ice.

So Allashua got out her line and her hook. She walked over to a large crack in the ice and started to fish. Right away a fish grabbed the hook and Allashua pulled it up. She caught six fish in a row.

Allashua yelled, "I am the best fisherman in the world!"

And from behind her something said, with a voice that sounded like snow blowing over the ice, *"The best you may be, but the smartest you are not."*

Allashua turned around. There, between her and the shore, were the Qallupilluit. They looked at her and said, *"Have you seen the child who said Qallupilluit have dirty noses?"*

"Oh, no, Qallupilluit. I have seen no such child, and besides, your noses are very pretty."

"Have you seen the child who said we smell like a dead whale in the summertime?"

"Oh, no, Qallupilluit. I have seen no such child, and besides, you smell very nice, just like flowers in the summer."

"Have you seen the child who yelled, 'Qallupilluit, Qallupilluit can't catch me'?"

"Oh, no, Qallupilluit. I have seen no such child, and besides, my mother says that you can catch whatever you want to."

"Right," said the Qallupilluit. *"We catch whatever we want to, and what we want to catch right now is you."*

One grabbed Allashua by her feet and dragged her down, down, under the sea ice to where the Qallupilluit live.

The sea water stung Allashua's face like fire. Allashua held her breath and the Qallupilluit gathered around her and sang, with voices that sounded like snow blowing over the ice:

> *Human child, human child*
> *Ours to have, ours to hold.*
> *Forget your mother, forget your father;*
> *Ours to hold under the ice.*

Allashua let out her breath and yelled, "My brothers and sisters, my brothers and sisters; I'll bring them all to the sea ice."

For a moment nothing happened, and then the Qallupilluit threw Allashua up out of the sea into the cold wind of the ice and said, *"A promise is a promise. Bring your brothers and sisters to the sea ice and we will let you go."*

Allashua began to run up the long, snow-covered path that led to her home. As she ran, her clothes started to freeze. She ran more and more slowly, until she fell to the ground. And that is where Allashua's father found her, almost at the back door, frozen to the snow.

Allashua's father gave a great yell, picked up Allashua and carried her inside. He tore off Allashua's icy clothes and put her to bed. Then the father and mother got under the covers and hugged Allashua till she got warm.
After an hour Allashua asked for some hot tea. She drank ten cups of hot tea with lots of sugar and said, "I went to the cracks in the sea ice."

"Ah, ah," said her family, "not so smart."
"I called the Qallupilluit nasty names."
"Ah, ah," said her family, "dumber still."
"I promised to take my brothers and sisters to the cracks in the sea ice. I promised to take them all to the Qallupilluit."

"Ah, ah," said her family, "a promise is a promise." Then her mother and father made some tea and they sat and drank it, and didn't say anything for a long time.

From far down the snow-covered path that led to the sea, the Qallupilluit began calling, *"A promise is a promise. A promise is a promise. A promise is a promise."*

The mother looked at her children and said, "I have an idea. Do exactly as I say. When I start dancing, all of you follow Allashua to the cracks in the sea ice."

And the children all whispered to each other, "Ah, ah, why will our mother dance? This is not a happy time."

Allashua's mother went out the back door and yelled, "Qallupilluit, Qallupilluit, come and talk with me."

And they did come, right up out of the cracks in the sea ice. Up the long, snow-covered path to the sea they came, and stood by the back door. It was a most strange thing, for never before had the Qallupilluit left the ocean.

The mother and father cried and yelled and asked for their children back, but the Qallupilluit said, "A promise is a promise."

The mother and father begged and pleaded and asked for their children back, but the Qallupilluit said, "A promise is a promise."

Finally Allashua's mother said, "Qallupilluit, you have hearts of ice; but a promise is a promise. Come and join us while we say good-bye to our children."

Everyone went inside. First the mother
gave her children some bread. She said to the
Qallupilluit, "This is not for you." But the
Qallupilluit said, *"We want some too."* The
mother gave the Qallupilluit some bread, and
they liked it a lot.

Then the mother gave each of her children
a piece of candy. She said to the Qallupilluit,
"This is not for you." But the Qallupilluit said,
"We want some too." The mother gave the
Qallupilluit some candy, and they liked it a lot.

Then the father started to dance. He said to the Qallupilluit, "This is not for you." The Qallupilluit said, "We have never danced. We want to dance." And they all started to dance. First they danced slowly and then they danced fast, and then they started to jump and yell and scream and dance a wild dance. The Qallupilluit liked the dancing so much that they forgot about children.

Finally the mother started to dance, and when the children saw their mother dancing, they crawled out the back door and ran down the long, snowy path that led to the sea. They came to the cracks in the sea ice and Allashua whispered, "Qallupilluit, Qallupilluit, here we are."

Nothing happened.
Then all the children said, "Qallupilluit, Qallupilluit, here we are."
Nothing happened.
Then all the children yelled, as loud as they could, "Qallupilluit, Qallupilluit, here we are!"

Nothing happened, and they all went back to the land and sat on a large rock by the beach.

Two minutes later the Qallupilluit ran screaming down the path and jumped into their cracks in the ice. Allashua stood up on the rock and said, "A promise is what you were given and a promise is what you got. I brought my brothers and sisters to the sea ice, but you were not here. A promise is a promise."

The Qallupilluit yelled and screamed and pounded the ice till it broke. They begged and pleaded and asked to have the children, but Allashua said, "A promise is a promise." Then the Qallupilluit jumped down to the bottom of the sea and took their cracks with them, and the whole ocean of ice became perfectly smooth.

Then the mother and father came walking down the long, snowy path to the ocean. They hugged and kissed each one of their children, even Allashua. The father looked at the flat ocean and said, "We will go fishing here, for Qallupilluit have promised never to catch children with their parents, and a promise is a promise."

Then they all did go fishing, quite happily. Except for

Allashua. She had been too close to the Qallupilluit and could still hear them singing, with voices that sounded like blowing snow:

Human child, human child
Ours to have, ours to hold.
Forget your mother, forget your brother;
Ours to hold under the ice.

A Qallupilluq is an imaginary Inuit creature, somewhat like a troll, that lives in Hudson Bay. It wears a woman's parka made of loon feathers and reportedly grabs children when they come too near cracks in the ice.

The Inuit traditionally spend a lot of time on the sea ice, so the Qallupilluit were clearly invented as a means to help keep small children away from dangerous crevices.

Michael Kusugak, thinking back to his childhood in the Arctic, made up a story about his own encounter with the Qallupilluit. He sent it to Robert Munsch, who had stayed with Michael's family while telling stories in Rankin Inlet, N.W.T. *A Promise is a Promise* is a result of their collaboration.

386

The Munsch for Kids series:

The Dark
Mud Puddle
The Paper Bag Princess
The Boy in the Drawer
Jonathan Cleaned Up—Then He Heard a Sound
Murmel, Murmel, Murmel
Millicent and the Wind
Mortimer
The Fire Station
Angela's Airplane
David's Father
Thomas' Snowsuit
50 Below Zero
I Have to Go!
Moira's Birthday
A Promise is a Promise
Pigs
Something Good
Show and Tell
Purple, Green and Yellow
Wait and See
Where is Gah-Ning?
From Far Away
Stephanie's Ponytail

––––––––––

Munschworks: The First Munsch Collection
Munschworks 2: The Second Munsch Treasury
Munschworks 3: The Third Munsch Treasury
Munschworks 4: The Fourth Munsch Treasury

––––––––––

Many Munsch titles are available in French and/or
Spanish. Please contact your favorite supplier.